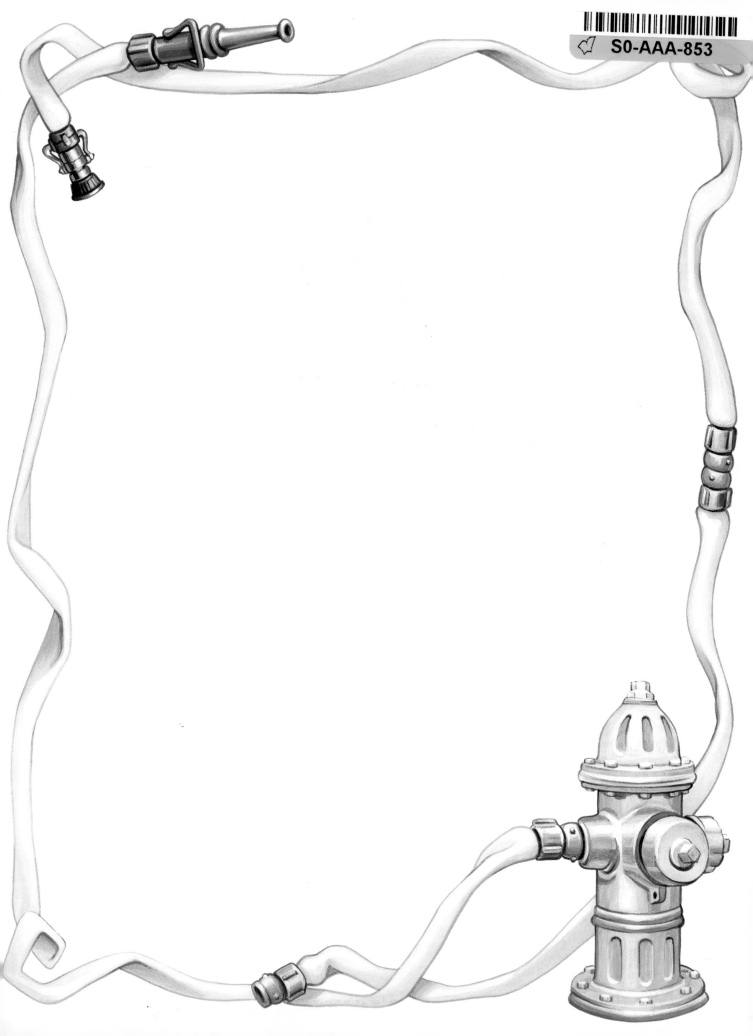

ISBN 1-58987-019-0

Published in 2004 by Kindermusik International, Inc.

Do-Re-Me & You! is a trademark of Kindermusik International, Inc.

Printed in Mexico
First Printing, February 2004

# The Kindertown Fire Brigade

# The Kindertown Fire Brigade

by Harold P. Gershenson

illustrated by Christopher Mills

When the Fourth of July parade came through the town,
Robbie Raccoon was clearly the proudest around.
He wore his blue uniform covered in braid
As head of the Kindertown Fire Brigade.

3

The engine appeared, and the air filled with cheers
As the whole town applauded the brave volunteers.
They roared their approval and sang out a song
When the cherry-red truck passed through the throng:

"Oh, those brave local heroes,
They're never afraid.
It's the Kindertown Volunteer Fire Brigade!"          5

The parade headed east toward the local fairground,
Where wonderful rides, games, and food would be found.
Among those attending there were quite a few
Who looked forward to trying Bernadette Bear's Hot
   Barbecue.

6

But through the commotion, an alarm was sounding.
Potter Parrot came flying, his heart loudly pounding.
He landed on Robbie and loudly exclaimed,
"The barbecue's burning. The tent is aflame!"

"It's Bernadette's restaurant! Oh, what a disaster!
Hurry, come quickly, before it grows vaster."
The team jumped into action—no need to persuade
The Kindertown Volunteer Fire Brigade.

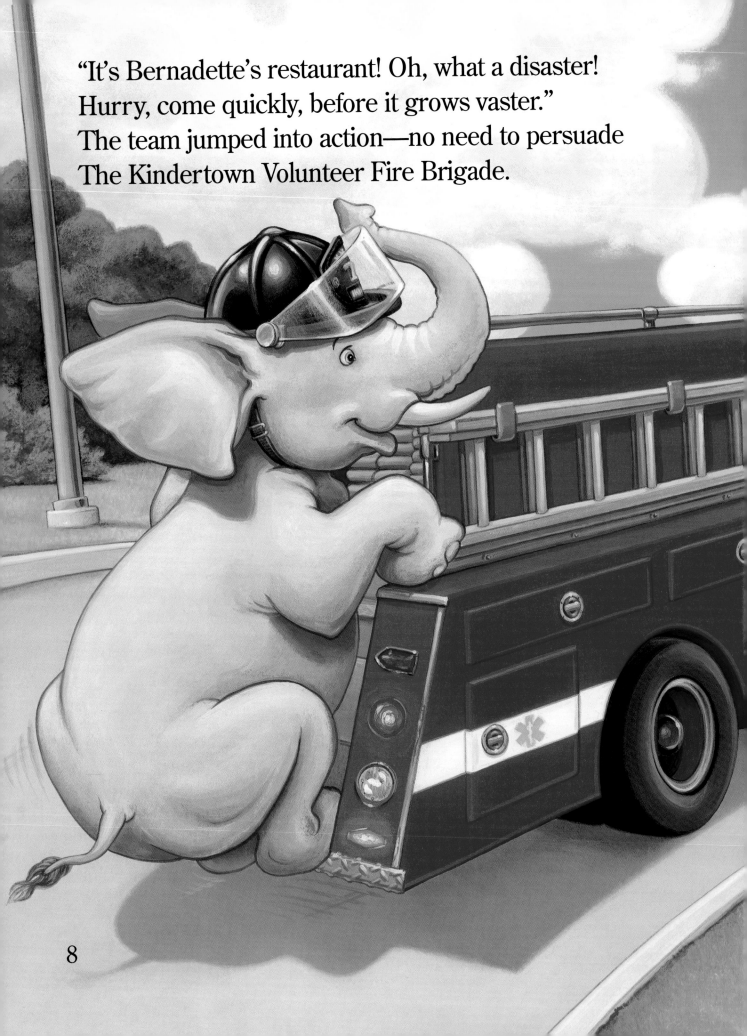

8

The truck raced with such speed that all were astounded,
And the crowd made way when the siren was sounded.
The crew arrived to see the barbecue blazing,
So they rushed to their posts—the team was amazing!

10

Eleanor Elephant took a big drink.
She loaded her trunk, right up to the brink.
Mighty Eleanor blew a glorious cascade,
And showered the Kindertown Fire Brigade!

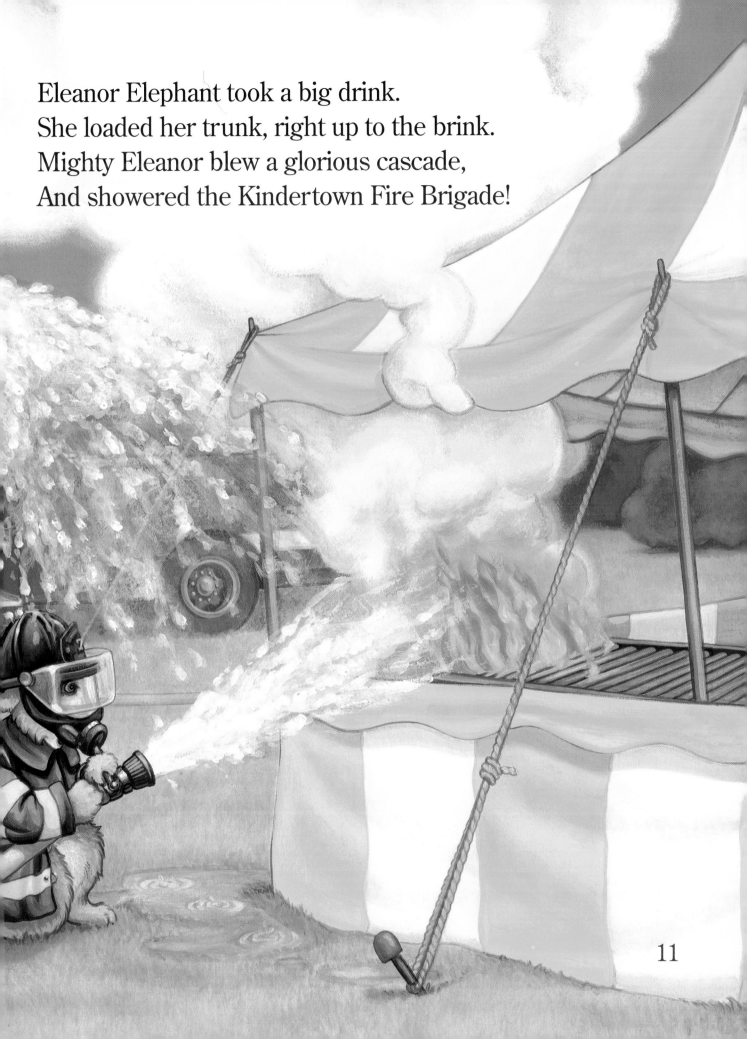

Sherman Shepherd kept the crowd in control;
He marched back and forth on a careful patrol.
He barked, a bit gruffly, and loudly he boomed,
"Make way! Stand back! Give the firefighters room!"

13

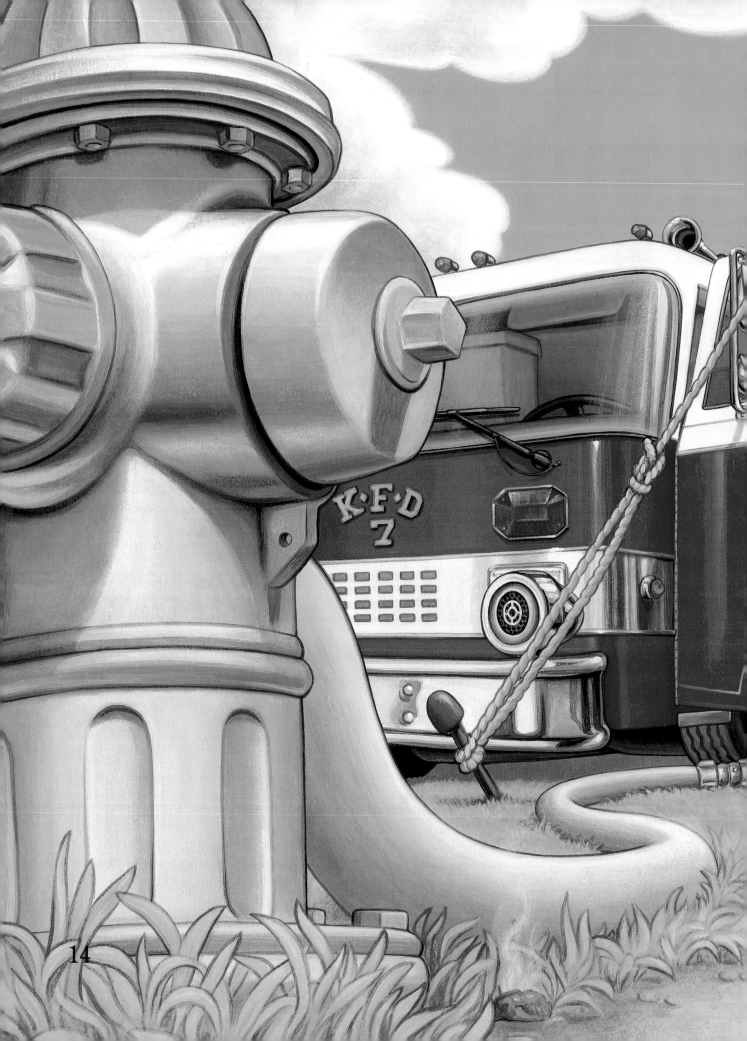

14

Ganymede Grasshopper, the crew's smallest member,
Dutifully hopped after each escaped ember,
And courageously spat on each glowing spark
Till it flickered, faded, and finally went dark.

After Bernadette was rescued, she saw she was bleeding—
And she fainted away, her heart quickly beating.
Robbie bellowed, "Bernadette, don't be dismayed!
You've been rescued by the Kindertown Fire Brigade."

17

Orton Octopus, the emergency medical technician,
Immediately stepped in and made a decision.
He bandaged Bernadette handily because he knew first aid,
As does the entire Kindertown Fire Brigade.

20

Everyone helped to clean up the mess—
Except Robbie, of course, who met with the press.
Bernadette got busy and served lemonade
To the Kindertown Volunteer Fire Brigade.

The fair started over with games and with rides,
With wild roller coasters and giant water slides.
The carnival lasted all the day long,
And as evening approached, everyone still
    hummed the song:

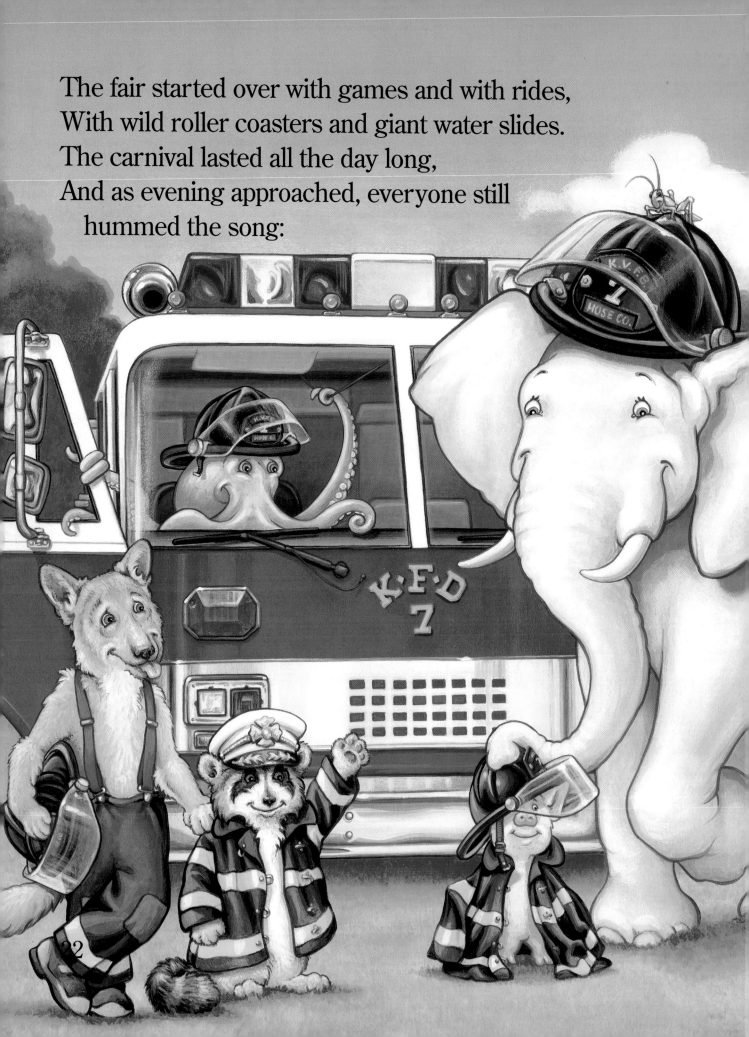

"Oh, those brave local heroes,
They're never afraid.
It's the Kindertown Volunteer Fire Brigade!"

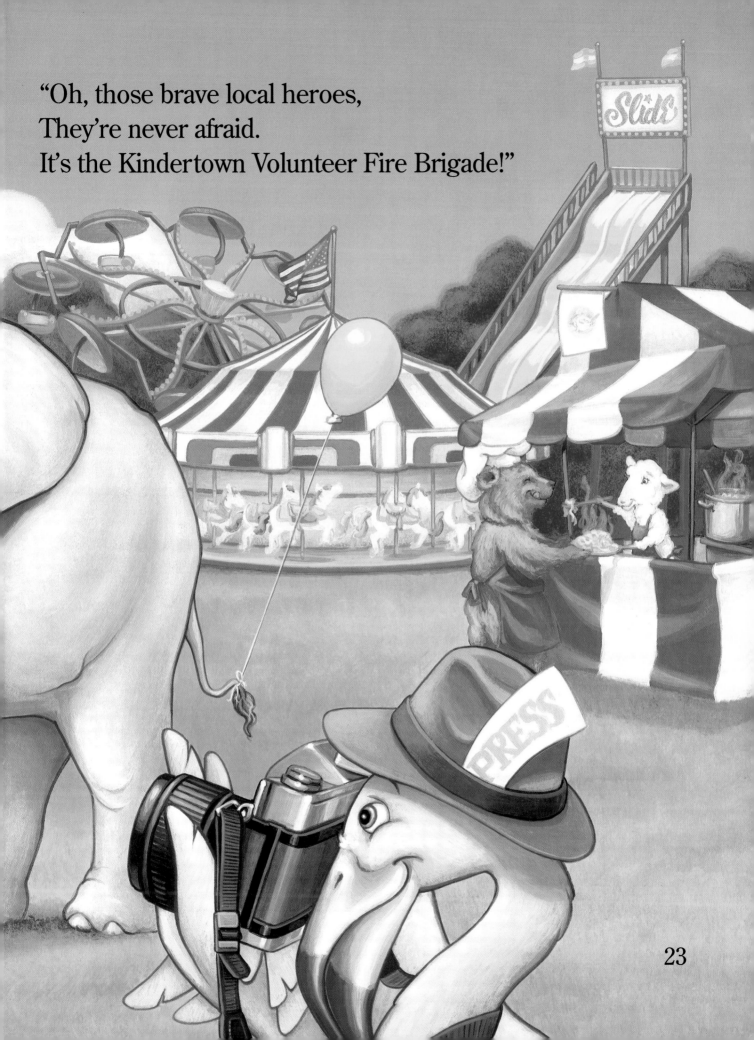

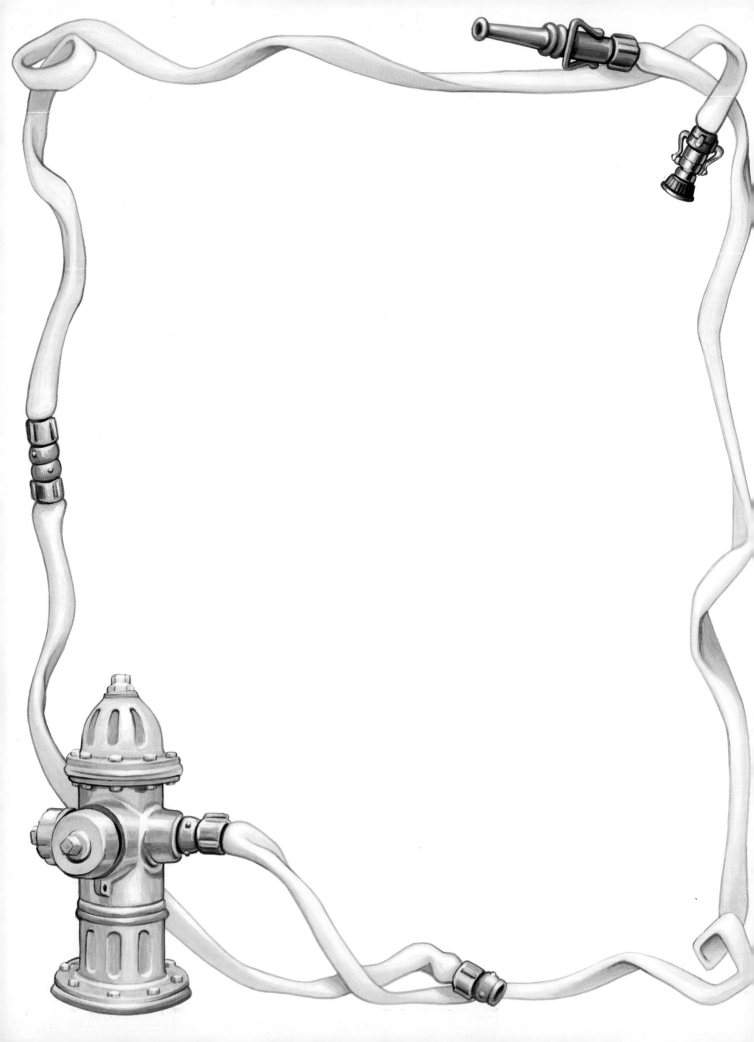